Lizzie McGuire

On the Job

Adapted by Leslie Goldman
Based on the series created by Terri Minsky
Part One is based on a teleplay written
by Nina G. Bargiel & Jeremy J. Bargiel.
Part Two is based on a teleplay written
by David Blum & Stacy Kramer.

Watch it on
DISNEY CHANNEL   abc Kids

DISNEY PRESS

VOLO

New York

PART ONE

CHAPTER ONE

Lizzie McGuire had it all worked out. She'd practiced in the mirror that morning, with her friends during lunch, and even after school. When she got home, she was happy to find her parents right where she wanted them—in the kitchen, making dinner. Her mom stood over a bubbling stew, and her dad was on salad duty, with knife and red pepper in hand.

"Hey, honey, how was school today?" Mrs. McGuire asked.

Lizzie cautiously approached her parents and put on her best "I'm your perfect daughter" smile. "Oh, school was wonderful. Did you guys have a good day?"

"It was okay," said Mr. McGuire.

"Yeah, it was just fine." Mrs. McGuire glanced at Lizzie, suspiciously.

"Oh, look." Lizzie beamed at her parents. "You're making your famous stroganoff. Oh, it's my favorite!"

"Are you in trouble, or do you want something?" Mrs. McGuire asked flatly.

"Oh, um . . ." Not expecting her parents to read her so well, Lizzie was kind of thrown off guard.

i knew the stroganoff was going too far. Last time, i tried to feed it to the dog. And we don't even have a dog.

"Well, you know, Mom, Dad. I'm . . . I'm getting older now, and I have a lot more needs. And I don't want to bug you guys every single time that I need to buy something, so, um, um . . ." Lizzie took a deep breath. Now or never, she told herself. It was time for the clincher. "I want a raise on my allowance."

How can you argue with that?

"No," Lizzie's parents said at the exact same time.

i guess that's how.

Okay, time to change tactics, Lizzie thought.

"But all of my friends got raises!" she argued.

> Give 'em the sad eyes. They can't say "no" to the sad eyes.

Lizzie blinked and looked at her parents with her trademark pleading puppy-dog eyes.

But Mrs. McGuire wasn't falling for it. "Oh, enough with the sad eyes," she said.

"Listen, if there's something you really need, just ask us," Mr. McGuire explained, in the logical, matter-of-fact tone that drove Lizzie crazy. "We'll get it for you."

"You know, that's just it, Dad! I don't want to have to ask anymore," Lizzie said. "I'm not a little kid. I need freedom."

"Well," said Mrs. McGuire, "when you

start earning money of your own, then you can be free with that. But until then, you have to manage with your allowance the way that it is."

"Fine," Lizzie huffed, unable to imagine the conversation having gone any worse. She stormed off, feeling depressed with a capital *D*.

> Yeah, well, your stroganoff tastes like an old shoe! An old, smelly, burnt shoe!

That night, Lizzie met her two best friends, Gordo and Miranda, at their favorite cybercafé, the Digital Bean. "And they said no about raising my allowance. Just like . . . just like *that*. Like, 'no,'" Lizzie complained.

"Well, did they say why?" Miranda asked,

as the three friends sat down at a table in the back of the Bean.

"I think it's because they want complete and total control over my life," Lizzie said. "Forever."

"Not forever," Gordo pointed out. "Just until you turn eighteen. You've only got a couple more years to go."

A couple more years? Don't I get time off for good behavior?

Lizzie felt rotten. "I just hate running to them for every little thing."

As Miranda nodded her head in agreement, she noticed a sign by the cash register. It read BUSBOY WANTED. "Lizzie, you could get a job," she said.

Lizzie went on talking as if she hadn't even heard Miranda. "When I'm at the mall and I want a pair of jeans, I want to buy them."

Miranda pointed to the sign and raised her voice. "Lizzie, you could get a job."

"I need independence and freedom," Lizzie went on. "But no, they won't let me have that."

When Gordo glanced up, he noticed the sign, too. "Lizzie, you could get a job," he said.

"A job?" Lizzie looked at Gordo like he was some sort of genius, which wasn't exactly a stretch. He was sort of one of the smartest kids in school. "What a great idea. I could get a job."

It was only when Miranda slumped over and dropped her head onto her arms that Lizzie noticed her. "Oh, I'm sorry. Were you saying something, Miranda?" Lizzie asked.

Miranda banged her head against her arms a few times before answering. "Huh? Oh, no.

I think getting a job is a great idea." Looking up, she pointed to the busboy sign yet again. "I think they're looking for a new busboy."

i can clear plates. i do that at home for free!

"I could be the new busboy!" said Lizzie, as she smoothed down her hair. "How do I look?"

"You look like a busboy," said Gordo, encouragingly.

"Okay," Lizzie said. She was a little bit nervous. She'd never had a job before—not a real one that didn't involve washing cars for world peace or manning the "Save the Rain Forest" bake sale cash register, anyway. Still, the blue sign said help was wanted here, and Lizzie wanted to help.

"Go get 'em," said Miranda.

Lizzie glanced at her friends hopefully and then headed to the counter.

She returned a few minutes later with a huge grin and the BUSBOY WANTED sign. "Looks like there's a new busboy in town!" Lizzie said.

McGuire's batting a thousand on the job front.

"So when do you start?" Gordo asked.

"I start tomorrow," Lizzie answered. This was way too cool.

"But I thought we were all supposed to hang at the mall tomorrow," Miranda said.

"Oh, well, we can hang here instead. It'll be fun," Lizzie replied.

"Are you sure?" Gordo asked. "We don't want to get you in trouble."

"Oh, no," Lizzie said. "I think it'll be fine. Plus, I think I can swing some free drinks for my friends."

Gordo's eyes widened. "Free?" he asked. "Free is my favorite number."

Back at the house, Matt and his friend Reggie were playing catch in the backyard. Well, Reggie was playing, anyway. Matt just stood there, staring off into space. When Reggie lobbed the football, it sailed right past Matt, who didn't even blink.

"Oh! Matt, is something up with you?" Reggie jogged past Matt to retrieve the football, which had landed in the bushes. "You didn't even notice I threw the ball."

"Oh," said Matt sadly.

"Dude, I know something's wrong. Even Lanny said you've been awful quiet lately." That really said something. Their friend

Lanny was quieter than a mime. When he walked, you couldn't even hear his footsteps.

Matt slumped down in a wicker chair. He hadn't been this depressed since he'd faked being sick and his mom had forced him to eat three bowls of beet soup. Sighing, he decided to come clean to his friend. "It's just . . . Reggie, I don't think Melina wants to be friends with me anymore."

"I thought things were good," Reggie said, more than a little confused. "She hasn't gotten you into trouble for days."

"Exactly," Matt said. "And Jared Ferguson has been in detention for nearly a week now. It doesn't take a genius to put two and two together." Matt rested his chin against his knuckles and slumped his shoulders. "Melina's moved on."

"You're better off without her, man," Reggie said.

Matt knew Reggie was trying to make him feel better, but it wasn't working. Yes, Melina was ignoring him, but Matt's problems were bigger than that. "It's just, I don't understand girls."

"Nobody understands girls," Reggie said. "Except, maybe, a girl." Suddenly, a huge smile broke out on Reggie's face.

Matt knew his buddy was on to something. "Talk to me," he said.

"Maybe you need to talk to a girl," Reggie suggested.

"But I don't know any," Matt argued.

"What about Lizzie?" asked Reggie.

"Ewww!" Matt made a face. "Lizzie's not a girl. She's my sister."

"But she's the closest thing you've got," Reggie reminded Matt.

Matt rested his chin on both knuckles. "So, *this* is what rock bottom looks like."

CHAPTER TWO

The next morning, Lizzie wolfed down her breakfast and picked up her plate right away.

Mrs. McGuire yelled out, "Hey, Matt! Hurry up, honey, or you're gonna be late for school!" Then, turning to Lizzie, she said, "Sweetheart, leave all that."

"Oh! It's no problem, Mom," Lizzie answered brightly, thinking she could use the practice. She picked up her dad's plate of bacon and eggs, not noticing he was still in the process of eating.

Mr. McGuire held his fork in midair, and stared hungrily at the plate in Lizzie's hand. "That's okay, I was nearly done, anyway," he said.

Mrs. McGuire blinked at Lizzie, curiously. "Okay," she said. "You've been good for two days in a row. What have you done?"

Lizzie was so excited, she could hardly stand still. "Um, okay. I got a job!"

"A job?" asked Mr. and Mrs. McGuire at the same time. They were so good at responding in synch, Lizzie wondered if they practiced their reactions beforehand.

"Yeah," Lizzie said, proudly. "I am the new busboy at the Digital Bean."

Mrs. McGuire looked at Lizzie, concerned. "Well, honey. I think you should've talked to us before getting a job."

"But now I don't have to ask you guys for money." Turning to her dad, she said, "And now you don't have to raise my allowance. It's a win-win situation."

"But, Lizzie," Mr. McGuire said, still eyeing his half-finished breakfast that hovered in front of him in Lizzie's hand. "Work is a huge responsibility." He lunged his fork at his eggs, but they were out of reach.

"Yeah, you have your homework and your friends and your chores. I mean, it's a lot to handle," said Mrs. McGuire.

"But, Mom," Lizzie said. "It's just a busboy job. I mean, I'll clean some tables, I'll see Gordo and Miranda, and I'll do my homework in between."

Mr. and Mrs. McGuire exchanged glances. It was another thing they were great at—talking to each other without actually exchanging words. Lizzie just waited.

After what seemed like ages, Mrs. McGuire turned to Lizzie and said, "I still think it's a lot to take on . . . but you know what, you're old enough to make your own decisions, so—"

"Thanks, Mom! Thanks, Dad," said Lizzie. "I can totally handle this."

"Welcome to the rat race," Mr. McGuire said, as he took back his eggs.

Lizzie headed off to school, so excited she was practically bouncing.

As she left, Matt walked into the kitchen. "Mom, Mom, where's Lizzie?" he asked, in a panicky voice.

"She just left," Mr. McGuire said.

"Oh, I really needed to talk to her," Matt said, very disappointed.

Mrs. McGuire said, "Oh, well, you can talk to me, sweetie."

"Sorry, Mom," said Matt. "But I need to talk to a girl."

As Matt left the kitchen, Mr. McGuire chuckled quietly.

CHAPTER THREE

Lizzie's first shift at the Digital Bean was going great. After she served a customer a muffin, she straightened her blue apron, and then sat down at the counter. I just served my first muffin, she thought. This is so cool!

This job thing rocks! i'm free! i'm independent! No one tells me what to do!

Just then, Lizzie's manager, a tough-talking

woman who was about ten years older than she, walked up and placed a purple paper napkin and a fork and knife on the counter. "Lizzie, front and center! I need you to roll silverware."

No problem, Lizzie thought, as she swiftly rolled the silverware and handed it back to her manager. Ha! If I had known working would be so easy, she thought, I would have gotten a job years ago!

Lizzie imagined all the cool things at the mall she'd be able to buy now. New jeans were just the beginning. There were jewel-encrusted hair clips and some dangly earrings, not to mention that cute zebra-striped tank top. Maybe she'd even get something nice for her mom.

"Impressive," the manager said, interrupting Lizzie's brief daydream. "Now you can turn pro." Lizzie's boss pointed to an enormous heap of silverware that was piled at the end of the counter.

With no choice, Lizzie got to work. Fifty minutes later, her fingers were stiff from silverware rolling, and she thought to herself that if she had to touch another fork, she'd run for the door, screaming in terror.

When her manager approached again, Lizzie asked, "Oh, what now?" in a weary voice.

"You're done for the day," the manager told her.

"Really?" Lizzie asked hopefully.

"No," the manager said. "But that gets them every time. Now, you're going to take all the rolled silverware and put it on the floor."

"Great." Lizzie tried to remember why she had been so excited about being a busboy. But nothing was coming to her.

As she lifted the tray full of rolled silverware, she realized that it was way too heavy. It was also a bit unbalanced. Suddenly, the tray tipped over, and all of the silverware went tumbling to the floor.

"Lizzie, just a hint," the manager said. "When I said, 'put it on the floor,' I didn't really mean 'on the floor.'"

"Yeah," said Lizzie. "I got it."

"Good," said the manager. "And I'm gonna need you to roll some more silverware."

Lizzie rested her head in her hands and moaned.

Half an hour later, Matt showed up at the Digital Bean. He sat down on a stool and said to the waitress at the end of the bar, "Juice. No ice. And keep 'em coming."

"Excuse me, worm," said Lizzie. "I don't pick up after you at home, and I don't plan on picking up after you here! Okay? So, don't make a mess."

As his third juice slid down the counter,

Matt grabbed it and downed it in one gulp. "Lizzie, I can't believe I've sunk this low, but I really need to talk to you."

Lizzie suddenly became serious. Even though Matt was an annoying worm, he *was* still her brother. "Matt, what's it about?"

"You see, it's about Melina. She's, uh . . ."

Before Matt could spit out the tragic news, Lizzie's boss showed up. "Uh, Lizzie? What are you doing?"

Lizzie looked at her, wondering why she was asking such an obvious question. "I'm talking to my little brother," she said. "Can I get a second?"

"What do *you* think?" the manager asked.

Whoops, thought Lizzie. "I think that I'm not being paid to talk to my brother," she covered.

"You're psychic," the manager said, pointing over her shoulder toward a dark corner of the café. "So, you already know the ketchup bottles need to be refilled."

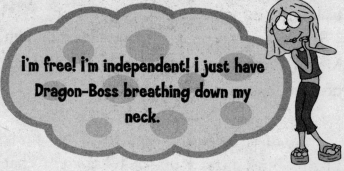

i'm free! i'm independent! i just have Dragon-Boss breathing down my neck.

"Okay." Lizzie walked off toward a table that was filled with a whole army of ketchup bottles—and they were ready to attack!

As she got to work, Miranda and Gordo entered the café.

"Hey, Matt," Gordo said.

"Uh, where's Lizzie?" Miranda asked.

"Over there." Matt, motioned toward the land of the empty ketchup bottles.

"How's her first day?" Gordo asked.

They watched as Lizzie inspected and then

shook a ketchup bottle. It didn't seem to be empty, so she stared into the opening and squeezed it a little. This turned out to be a huge mistake, because as she did so, a huge glop of ketchup landed on her face.

"Pretty much like that," said Matt. "Juice me," he said to the waitress. Seconds later, she slid another glass to Matt, who caught it expertly.

Miranda glanced at the many empty glasses on the counter. "Uh, you're hitting the juice pretty hard there, aren't you, Matt?"

Matt said, "You wouldn't understand. You see, I need to talk to a girl, but Lizzie's the only one I know, and she's busy."

"Matt? I'm a girl," said Miranda.

Matt looked at Miranda, and it was like he was seeing her for the very first time. She wasn't just Lizzie's friend. She was Lizzie's friend with soft brown eyes, and a cute, pink, furry thing in her hair. Suddenly, his day seemed brighter. "Hey, you are, aren't you?" he said.

"Nothin' gets past you, does it?" Gordo asked.

Matt ignored him and turned his attention to Miranda. "You see, it's about Melina. She's getting someone else into trouble. Someone who's not me."

"And?" asked Miranda, not really seeing the problem.

Matt downed another glass of juice, slammed his hand against the counter, and blurted out, "Juice me."

He turned back to Miranda. "I think she's moved on," he explained.

Lizzie's little bro was already into girls? Miranda looked at Gordo, not knowing what to say.

Gordo stifled a laugh. "I'm gonna let you handle this one," he said.

Miranda turned back to Matt. "You know, Melina doesn't realize how good she has it."

"What do you mean?" Matt asked.

"Matt, you're a great kid," Miranda replied.

This was news to Matt. "I am?" he asked.

Miranda nodded. "Totally."

"You really think so?" Matt asked again, not really believing what he was hearing.

"Absolutely," said Miranda. "And if Melina can't see that, then she's not worth it."

Matt stared at Miranda, who was looking less and less like his sister's best pal and more and more like a supermodel.

"Not bad," Gordo whispered to Miranda, genuinely impressed with her advice.

"Wow," Matt said. Suddenly his heart felt lighter and kind of fluttery. "You really think I'm a great kid?"

"Yeah, I really do." Miranda answered, sincerely. "And there are plenty of other girls out there who'd be lucky to go out with you."

"Wow, thanks." Matt suddenly realized, after all this time, that Miranda wasn't just pretty—she was totally hot!

"Sure, no problem." Miranda shrugged.

Just then, Lizzie yelped loud enough for the entire café to hear.

"Maybe we should catch up with Lizzie later. . . ." Gordo said, motioning toward Lizzie who looked like she'd been attacked by a ketchup-spitting monster. Her once-clean apron was now red and sticky. She had ketchup in her hair, ketchup on her face, and ketchup underneath her fingernails.

Gordo, Miranda, and Matt cringed at the sight. ". . . when she's not so tomato-y," Gordo added.

"You could come over after dinner." Matt suggested eagerly, assuming his sister would be ketchup-free by then.

"Cool," said Miranda, totally oblivious to Matt's drooling over her. "Tell Lizzie we'll see her then."

As Gordo and Miranda left the Digital Bean, Matt looked after Miranda with puppy-dog eyes. "It's a date," he said with a sigh.

CHAPTER FOUR

Later that day, Gordo, Lizzie, and Miranda walked through the McGuires' backyard. Little did they know that someone was watching them from inside.

"So how was your first day in the working world?" Miranda asked.

"Besides sticky," Gordo added.

"Totally busy," said Lizzie. "I didn't stop working the whole time I was there."

Lizzie's job was way different than she'd thought it'd be. She figured she'd be clearing the occasional table and filling a water glass here and there, while getting paid to chill with her friends. But back in the real world, Lizzie's day was insane. If she wasn't rolling silverware, she was mopping the floor. If she wasn't mopping the floor, she was clearing plates. And if she wasn't clearing plates, she was filling bottles of sticky, old ketchup.

Her feet ached, and her hands were all prune-y and wrinkled from washing dishes. She just wanted to earn some cash to buy some clothes, and maybe the new scent she tried at the mall, but the only perfume she was wearing now was eau de ketchup!

Gordo noticed someone peeking out from inside the house, but when he looked back, the blinds closed. Thinking it must have been Lizzie's mom or dad, he turned his attention back to Lizzie's comment. "Isn't that the definition of a job?" he asked.

"Uh, yeah, but I didn't think it would be so much . . ." Lizzie paused as she tried to come up with the perfect word.

"Work?" Gordo asked. He looked up again, and this time he was sure someone was spying on them. He saw Lizzie's brother peeking over the half-door from inside the house, but then a second later, Matt was gone. Gordo shook his head.

Meanwhile, Lizzie and Miranda continued their conversation, completely oblivious to the fact that someone was watching them. "Yeah, but when payday comes around, you'll be swimming in cash," Miranda said, thinking, first Matt, now Lizzie—I give great advice!

"Exactly," said Lizzie, her spirits brightening a little.

Just then Matt rose up from behind a lawn chair, startling everyone so much that they screamed out in unison.

"Lizzie, Mom wants you in the kitchen," Matt said.

"Don't ever do that again, Matt!" Lizzie yelled. Turning to Gordo and Miranda, she softened her tone. "I'll be right back." To Matt she warned, "And don't bug my friends."

As Lizzie walked away, Matt handed Miranda a card. "Here," he said before darting off.

"Thanks," Miranda said, totally confused.

Gordo smiled. "I think Matt's over Melina."

"I know," Miranda nodded. "I give such good advice."

"No, no, you're missing my point, Miranda. He's over Melina because he's got a crush on you."

"Puh-lease," Miranda said, looking at Gordo like he was crazy. "This is *Matt*. He's just giving me a *thank-you* card."

"Yeah," said Gordo, knowing what was coming next.

Miranda opened the card. Inside was a picture of a couple holding hands—cute, except for one problem. That couple was Matt and Miranda! Matt had glued pictures of the two of them over the original couple's faces!

Miranda heard scary movie music playing in her head as it dawned on her that Lizzie's little brother *did* have a crush on her. A big, bad one, in fact. "Ahhhhhh!" she screamed in terror.

"I hate being right all the time," said Gordo, who was clearly enjoying this new turn of events. "So, when you and Matt get married, are you gonna move in here, or are you gonna get an apartment, or what?"

As she closed the card, Miranda just shuddered, trying to shake off her acute case of ickiness.

Gordo walked into the house, but Miranda opened the card again and gaped. There was her face, still glued right there next to Matt's. She was truly stunned by this horror of horrors. And looking at it was just as bad the second time around.

The Digital Bean was hopping the next afternoon, but Lizzie was too busy to enjoy it. She ran around, bussing tables, cleaning up messes, and rolling more silverware. Her shift had started just a couple of hours ago but she was already exhausted and counting the minutes till she could leave. Gordo was right. She'd had no idea an after-school job could be so much, er . . . work!

Miranda and Gordo walked in and scanned the place for an empty table. Gordo broke out his Hacky Sack and started kicking.

Lizzie marched over to them. "Hey, I'm off

in fifteen minutes, so just sit over there and don't order anything!"

She grabbed Gordo's Hacky Sack. "And Gordo, will you please stop this. Okay? You're gonna knock something over, and I'm gonna have to clean it up."

As Gordo and Miranda sat down, Miranda said, "Guess we can't talk to the new, working Lizzie."

"Probably not. But you've got the next-best thing," Gordo said, pointing to Matt, who had just rolled in on his scooter. "Your boyfriend."

"He is *not* my boyfriend," Miranda replied through gritted teeth.

Gordo looked at Matt's new license plate, which read MATT ❤ MRNDA.

"But he hearts you, Miranda!" Gordo joked.

As Miranda sat down, Matt scooted over.

Just when she thought it couldn't get any worse, she noticed he was sporting a large button with a picture of her face on it!

"Fancy meeting you here," Matt said. Then he glared at Gordo and said in a voice dripping with jealousy, "Gordo."

But Gordo didn't mind at all. He was having too much fun. "Hey, I like your button, man."

"Thanks," said Matt. "I made it myself."

This was way too much for Miranda—she was freaking out.

Matt, trying to be an attentive "boyfriend," asked, "Something wrong, sunshine?"

Sunshine? Miranda could barely speak. "I . . . I just need a drink."

"One drink, two straws. Comin' right up," said Matt as he sped off.

Miranda scowled at Gordo. "You could be a little more helpful, Gordo."

Gordo shrugged with pretend innocence. "What? I said I liked his button."

When Miranda narrowed her eyes at him, he said, "I'm sorry. It's just so . . . funny."

Gordo wasn't the only one enjoying his afternoon at the Digital Bean. Kate Sanders, the head cheerleader, and Claire Miller, the junior captain (aka Lizzie's two least favorite people), sat watching Lizzie like hawks. They were totally pleased with the fact that she was scrambling around like a cheerleader without her pom-poms. Deciding that Lizzie wasn't quite stressed enough, Kate knocked over Claire's strawberry smoothie. Pink goop oozed onto the table and dripped onto the floor. Lizzie spotted the mess and stomped over.

"Okay, which one of you did this?" she asked, angrily.

"It's called an accident, Lizzie," Kate said as she shot Lizzie a nasty look.

Around Kate and Claire, there is no such thing as an accident.

"Sure, it was an accident," Lizzie said sarcastically.

Just then, her manager walked over. "It'd be really nice if there was a busboy around to clean this up," she said. Glaring at Lizzie, she added, "Hey, look who's here."

"But they did it on purpose," Lizzie argued.

Kate looked up at the manager and blinked innocently. "Honestly, it was an accident."

"Lizzie," the manager said. "Get a rag.

Clean this up. And apologize to these customers."

Life was so unfair! Lizzie wanted to argue. "But, but . . ."

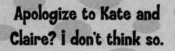

Apologize to Kate and Claire? i don't think so.

"Or I could put the BUSBOY WANTED sign back up," the manager replied.

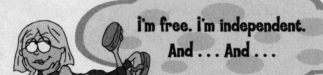

i'm free. i'm independent. And . . . And . . .

Lizzie looked from the manager to Kate and Claire. She wanted to throw up! "Sorry," she mumbled.

i don't know which is grosser— having to apologize to Kate and Claire, or cleaning melted smoothie off the floor.

Lizzie got a rag and started wiping up the mess, clearly grossed out.

"Oh, look," Claire cooed. "You missed a spot." Claire and Kate high-fived each other and flipped their hair over their shoulders.

And a few minutes later, Lizzie's shift was finally over.

CHAPTER FIVE

The alarm clock blared next to Lizzie's bed, but she felt like the buzzing was going off right between her ears. She couldn't believe it was Saturday morning already.

She'd been having the worst nightmare: She was a busboy at the Digital Bean, and she was covered in ketchup, and she had to clean up after Kate and Claire . . . oh, wait. . . . As Lizzie woke up, she realized that the night-mare was actually just her life!

She picked up her alarm clock and smothered

it with a pillow. Then she buried her head underneath another pillow.

Suddenly, she heard a knock on her door.

"Come in," Lizzie called.

Her dad walked into the room. It was Saturday and he was in jeans and a baseball cap, looking relaxed. Unlike Lizzie, who was wearing a too-tired-to-do-anything look on her face. "Hey, honey. Don't you have to work today?" her dad asked.

Lizzie answered sadly. "Yes."

"Let me rephrase this," Mr. McGuire said, gently. "Are you planning on going to work today?"

"I don't really have a choice," Lizzie mumbled from under her pillow.

Here it comes—the responsibility lecture.

"Of course you have a choice," said Mr. McGuire. "You could always quit."

Lizzie sat up. Was she hearing him right?

Who are you and what have you done with my real dad?

"Dad, I'm not gonna quit. Earning my own money makes me happy," Lizzie said.

"You don't look happy," Mr. McGuire observed, all too accurately.

"Well, that's why it's called a job," Lizzie reasoned. "Because it requires a little bit of work."

"Lizzie," her father answered. "The great thing about being a kid is that your only job is to get good grades, to hang out with your friends, and be a good kid. You've got those covered."

"Well, Dad, this is what I really want to be doing. I mean, I hate running to you guys for every little thing. I want to be independent."

"Okay. But independent is harder than it looks," Mr. McGuire said. "Listen—I'm your dad. You're supposed to ask me for stuff."

"Well, then can I ask you for a ride to work because I'm gonna be really late," Lizzie said.

"Okay," Mr. McGuire answered.

"Okay," Lizzie whispered, getting up.

"Yeah, she's going," Mr. McGuire called down to his wife.

Hearing that, Lizzie collapsed back into her bed for her last few seconds of rest for the day.

That afternoon, Miranda looked around her room, which was filled wall-to-wall with balloons—heart-shaped red ones, pink ones, orange ones, white ones, and yellow ones.

Some had pictures of Matt's face printed on them and some had pictures of Miranda's.

She pushed through the helium and rubber jungle, found her phone, and dialed frantically. "Gordo! Good! You're home. Okay, Matt's crush on me has gone totally loco," Miranda said, punching the psycho balloons out of the way.

"Ah," Gordo said, totally enjoying the moment. "Isn't that great?"

"No!" Miranda said. "It's horrible."

"Maybe for you," Gordo replied. "But for me, it's endlessly entertaining."

Before she could respond to her so-not-funny friend, Miranda had another call. "Ugh. Hang on, that's my other line."

Feeling completely stressed, Miranda clicked over and shouted, "Hello!" into the phone.

"I love the way you say hello," said a lovesick Matt, on the other end.

"Oh, Matt." Miranda's heart sank. "Hey, can you hang on a sec?"

"Till the end of time," Matt swooned.

Miranda clicked back over to Gordo. "It's Matt! What do I say?"

"I dunno—he's *your* boyfriend," Gordo said. "Talk about what you usually talk about."

"Not helping, Gordo," Miranda said between clenched teeth.

"So, uh, why don't you tell him you just want to be friends?" Gordo suggested, not adding that girls used that line on him all the time.

"Friends? I can do that." Miranda clicked back. "Matt," she said, as she pushed another balloon out of the way. "I'm so glad you called."

Matt took a deep breath and crossed his fingers. "Hey, I was wondering maybe if you wanted to go bike-riding later."

"Like, on a date?" Miranda asked. It was such a sweet gesture. She hated to shoot the kid down.

"Um, yes?" asked Matt.

"Uh, can you hang on?" Miranda clicked back to Gordo.

Meanwhile, Matt crossed his fingers and arms and toes and legs, in hopes that Miranda would say yes.

She pushed a balloon away from her head, exclaiming, "He just asked me out on a date!"

"So I guess the 'let's-just-be-friends' thing didn't work?" Gordo asked.

"Oh, Gordo, what do I say?"

Gordo shrugged. For once, he had no idea what to do. "Well, if you don't do something quick, you're gonna be Mrs. Matt McGuire."

Miranda rolled her eyes and clicked back to Lizzie's little brother. "Hey," she said.

"So will you go?" Matt asked, squinting his

eyes shut and crossing his arms and fingers again.

"Well . . . I . . . I mean . . ." Try as she might, Miranda just couldn't come up with a decent excuse. "Sure."

Matt dropped the phone and started doing a victory dance. "Yes! Yes! Yes!"

After Miranda hung up, she popped balloons left and right.

CHAPTER SIX

Back at the Digital Bean, Lizzie's day wasn't getting any better. The café was packed, and to make matters worse, Kate and Claire had front-row seats! Every time Lizzie walked by, they pointed and whispered, rolled their eyes, or just snickered.

A stuffy man in a tie banged his spoon on the table and motioned for Lizzie. "Could you get me another spoon, please?"

Lizzie looked down at the bagel on his plate, confused. "Why?" she asked.

"Because this spoon is dirty," the man said.

"Sir, you're eating a bagel," Lizzie pointed out. "You don't need a spoon to eat a bagel."

"I need a clean spoon," the man said, raising his voice as if Lizzie were hard of hearing.

"Okay, sir. I'll be right back," said Lizzie, tiredly.

As she walked toward the counter she noticed something fly through the air. A young kid was giggling as he smashed up a muffin and then threw the crumbs all over the *clean* floor. The *very* clean floor. The *very* clean floor Lizzie had *just* cleaned! Frustrated, but trying to keep her cool, she bent down and picked the crumbs up.

"Isn't he a cute kid?" the muffin boy's dad said with a smile.

Lizzie just shook her head. She grabbed a

spoon from the bin of clean silverware, went back to the lunatic bagel guy, and placed it on the table. "There you go, sir. There's your clean spoon."

"You just touched that spoon after cleaning the floor," said the man. "That spoon is dirty. I need a clean one."

Ignoring Kate and Claire's giggles, Lizzie went back to the counter to wash her hands. But before she got a chance to, her boss said, "Lizzie, the garbage won't take itself out."

"I'll be there in a second, okay?" Lizzie responded.

"Okay." The manager waited for literally one second and then said, "Now."

Now i know why no one else applied for this job.

The garbage was an overflowing mess. Lizzie crammed things down from the top.

Meanwhile, muffin boy continued to throw crumbs on the ground, and even worse, his dad was now doing the same thing. The spoon guy tapped his knife against the side of his plate and motioned Lizzie over again. Grabbing a clean spoon, she brought it to him. "There you go."

The spoon guy was horrified. "You just touched the garbage and didn't wash your hands! That spoon is dirty. I need a clean one."

Lizzie didn't have the patience to argue with him, so she walked to the sink, washed her hands, grabbed a spoon, and headed toward the table.

Seeing her approach, Claire spilled her raspberry smoothie onto the floor. Lizzie didn't notice and slipped, landing flat on her back. *Oof!*

"Oops," said Kate. "Sorry." Her voice could not have sounded any less apologetic.

"Accidents happen," Claire said, in an equally nasty tone.

Fuming mad and in a lot of pain, Lizzie got up off the ground. "You know what? No!"

i've had all i can stand, and i can't stand no more.

"Okay, listen up, that was not an accident. All right? And my job is hard enough without you two brats making it worse."

Hearing the commotion, the manager walked over. "Lizzie," she started.

But Lizzie interrupted. "And you see this mess? I'm not cleaning it up. I'm not cleaning up after anybody in this whole room!" She pointed to the muffin boy. "And you, little muffin boy! You see this right here? You eat this muffin or you put it in the trash can. But keep it off my clean floor." She walked over to the spoon guy. "And Mr. Spoon Boy? You don't need a spoon to eat a bagel." Lizzie grabbed the bagel and started waving it in front of his face. Then she shoved it into his mouth before he could say a word in protest. "I came here trying to do my job so I didn't have to ask my parents for money anymore. I want to be free, and I want to be independent! But no! Obviously, that's not gonna happen."

"Uh, Lizzie," said the manager.

"And you!" Lizzie spun around and pointed at her boss. "You're always telling me what to do, and always asking me for things! And that's not being free or independent at all! Now is it?"

"You're absolutely right," said the manager. "You done?"

"Yes," said Lizzie. "Yes, I feel a lot better now."

"I am so glad," said the manager with a small grin. "You're fired."

"Fired?" asked Lizzie. "I'm fired?"

"Eh, don't feel too bad," the manager said. "I go through three busboys a month."

When Kate and Claire burst into a fit of nasty giggles, Lizzie just glared.

But then she realized: no more sticky ketchup bottles, no more cleaning up after Claire and Kate, no more muffin boys, and no more rolling silverware. Maybe being fired wasn't so bad, after all. . . .

CHAPTER SEVEN

Gordo and Miranda walked through the McGuires' backyard. "Just like we practiced," Gordo coached.

Miranda repeated. "Matt, you're a really great kid but I think we should just be friends."

Gordo shook his head, sadly. "I can't believe you're gonna break Matt's heart."

Miranda shot him a glare. "You know what? You just want me to keep this going for your own sick amusement."

"Well, yeah," Gordo said. He'd thought that was obvious.

"Wait," said Miranda.

They walked inside to find Matt on the couch, playing a video game. Hearing them enter, he looked up. "Miranda, you're early. I thought we were going bike-riding later. I mean, I haven't even had time to wrap your present."

"Yeah, well, we need to talk," said Miranda.

"Is something wrong?" Matt asked.

"Well, kind of." Miranda squirmed, thinking this was so much harder than she'd thought it would be. She glanced at Gordo, remembering the speech they'd practiced. Opening her mouth, she found that the words wouldn't come out.

Misinterpreting the look, Matt narrowed his eyes at Gordo. "Is it someone else?" he asked.

Gordo said, "Uh, no. Don't worry. She's all yours."

"Gordo!" said Miranda, wondering whose side he was on. Turning to Matt she said, "Matt, no—there's no one else."

Matt grinned. "Phew! That's good 'cause I don't think I can return these." He held up a couple of T-shirts. Both pictured supersized Matt heads, and one had an arrow that read, I'M WITH . . .

Miranda gasped. "What do I say to that?" she whispered to Gordo.

"I say you go out with him." Gordo laughed. "Those shirts are pretty cool."

Miranda shot Gordo her "you're not helping at all" look. She realized she'd have to handle this on her own.

Just then, Melina entered the room. Looking back and forth between Miranda and Matt, she said, "So, the rumor is true?"

"Hello, Melina," Matt said, nervously.

"Listen," said Melina, shooting Miranda an icy glare. "Just because you can't find a guy your own age doesn't mean you can steal mine."

Miranda was so confused. What was going on?

"You're just a rebound girl!" Melina continued. "So keep your distance. 'Cause if anybody's gonna get Matt in trouble, it's gonna be me. Got it?"

Matt looked from Melina to Miranda, and then back to Melina again. "You really do like me!" Matt said.

"Let's go," Melina said.

Matt jumped off the couch as if it were on fire. "Sorry things didn't work out," he said to Miranda.

"Now!" shouted Melina.

"Coming, my angel," Matt sang.

He grabbed the shirts and followed Melina outside. "Look, I made these for you. . . ."

Miranda and Gordo were left standing in the McGuire living room, totally stunned. "Well, that was easy," Miranda said.

Gordo looked at her. "You do realize that you just got dumped by Matt."

Miranda gave him the evil eye. "We're not talking about this ever again. Especially to Lizzie."

"All right"—Gordo folded his arms over his chest and grinned—"rebound girl."

"That was talking about it," Miranda warned, through clenched teeth.

As they walked out, they ran into Lizzie.

"Hey, you guys," she said. "What are you doing here?"

"You know, it's a funny story," Gordo said, following Lizzie into the kitchen.

Miranda slapped the back of his head, and Gordo closed his mouth.

"So, how was your day?" Miranda asked.

"It was great." Lizzie coughed. "Until I got fired."

"Oh . . . well, what happened?" Miranda asked.

"You were caught drinking straight from the shake machine, weren't you?" Gordo said. When Lizzie and Miranda both shot him a crazy look, he shrugged his shoulders. "What? That's what I would've done."

"No," Lizzie explained. "I wasn't as polite as I should've been to the customers."

i think that qualifies for the understatement of the year.

"It wasn't pretty," Lizzie went on.

"So I take it the money train has stopped rolling," Gordo said.

"Gordo," Lizzie said. "I don't think that the money train ever took off from the station. Besides, if I'm always working, how am I gonna have time to spend the money?"

"Good point," Miranda said.

Lizzie looked at her friends. "So, what's up with you guys? I feel like I haven't seen you in days. What's been going on?" She walked to the fridge and opened it up.

Gordo was about to give Lizzie the 4-1-1 on the "Miranda-Matt-Melina love triangle" when Miranda shot him another warning look. "Nothing," he said. "Nothing at all."

"You guys hungry?" Lizzie asked as she peered into the fridge.

"Keep it zipped," Miranda said to Gordo under her breath.

Meanwhile Lizzie spotted a pink, heart-shaped cake in the fridge. She took it out and placed it on the counter. "Ooh, cake," she said, distractedly. She peered back inside for something to drink. "Milk?"

Miranda stared down at the cake, horrified. It read, "I ❤ Miranda." Gordo started to laugh, silently.

"Yeah," Miranda said. Since Lizzie's back was still turned, Miranda wiped the frosting off the top of the cake with her fingertips, smearing off her name and the rest of the message. Not knowing what else to do with the evidence, Miranda shoved it into her mouth.

Lizzie turned back around and stared at her friend, whose face was covered in pink frosting.

"Frosting's the best part," Miranda mumbled with her mouth full, grinning bashfully. Talk about eating your own words!

Lizzie looked at her friend's messy face. She wondered if some frosting had fallen on the floor or messed up the counter. She almost got ready to grab a rag to clean it up, but decided against it. Her days as a busboy were behind her for the time being. And she couldn't have been happier!

Lizzie McGUiRE

PART
TWO

CHAPTER ONE

After school on Thursday, Lizzie broke out her new candle-making kit and got started. Pale yellow wax bubbled on a double burner on the stove, and her can-shaped molds lined the counter. She smelled her two latest candles. One was purple, and one was red. Mmm . . . vanilla-scented bliss! Next she measured out wax for some blue and pink ones.

Mrs. McGuire was preparing dinner nearby, but took a break to peer over Lizzie's shoulder. "Honey, don't let that cloth get too close to that burner."

"I know, Mother." Lizzie glared at her mom, thinking, there's nothing worse than a backseat candle-maker. Still, she picked up the dishcloth and tossed it away from the stove.

Mrs. McGuire went back to pounding on a large slab of meat. "I'm sorry, I'm sorry. I know you're not a small child," she said to Lizzie.

The phone rang, and Mrs. McGuire answered it. "Hello? Oh, hey, Debby."

Lizzie dropped a new wick in the mushy wax as she listened to her mother's end of the conversation.

"Well if you can't baby-sit tomorrow night, you can't baby-sit." Mrs. McGuire smiled as she held the phone. "No, I'm not angry at you for calling me last minute. Okay, bye-bye," she said, sweetly. Hanging up, she went back to the meat. But this time she really pounded on it!

Lizzie raised her eyebrows but otherwise

ignored her mom's obvious attack on the poor cutlet.

A few moments later, Mr. McGuire and Matt came home from Matt's soccer practice. Matt, who was almost at eye level with the night's dinner, asked, "Why is Mom mad at the meat?"

"Oh, hi, honey," Mrs. McGuire said, easing up on her full-force thrashing. "How was practice?"

"Zachary Greenwald accidentally fell on a sprinkler head and had to get stitches," Matt said, sadly.

As Mrs. McGuire shuddered, Matt slowly smiled and said, "It was really cool."

"And Matt came very close to actually kicking the ball, didn't you, champ?" Mr. McGuire asked.

"Oh, yeah." Matt puffed out his chest proudly.

Mr. McGuire stood over him and mouthed silently, "No way!"

"Oh, Debby Gottschalk called," said Mrs. McGuire. "She can't baby-sit tomorrow night."

"Well, is there anyone else we can get?" Mr. McGuire asked. He'd been looking forward to a night out on the town all week and was clearly disappointed.

"Oh, oh," Lizzie chimed in. "Don't get that Olivia Skibbens. She makes us listen to country-western, nonstop." Lizzie shuddered as she had a nightmarish flashback to the time when she and Matt were forced to line dance in the living room, for two hours straight! She was so brainwashed by the twangy tunes that the next day at the mall she actually checked out a pair of cowboy boots!

Matt had a different fear. Making a face he said, "Not Mrs. Harvey. She smells dead."

"Well, we're not going for Tammy up the street, either," said Mrs. McGuire, as she remembered handing over stacks of cash at the end of a night, unhappily. "'Cause she makes more an hour than I do."

"No way we're going with Mrs. Jaffe," said Mr. McGuire. "Who lets a boy drink an entire quart of maple syrup?"

Matt grinned as he recalled that night. With his mind buzzing from the best sugar rush ever, he'd raced around the kitchen island, feeling like the winning car in the Indy 500! "I liked her," he said.

"Well, we've gotta find somebody," said Mrs. McGuire.

Suddenly, a perfect idea popped into Lizzie's head. She looked at her parents, hopefully, wondering how best to approach the topic. "Um, well, I was thinking . . . I was thinking maybe I could—"

But before she managed to say the words, her parents finished her sentence for her. "Baby-sit?" they asked at the exact same time, both sounding equally horrified.

Wow! They must have *both* read the "How to Be an Overprotective Parent" newsletter this month!

Mrs. McGuire said, "Honey, we've talked about this, you know, we just think you're . . ." Her voice trailed off as she gently tried to come up with the right words.

"You're too young," Mr. McGuire said, firmly. "No."

"When will I be old enough to trust? When I'm fifty?" Lizzie exclaimed.

"Maybe," Mr. McGuire answered. "We'll see." He walked over to the stove to check out dinner. "Where's Mrs. Doubtfire when you need her?" he wondered as he dipped his finger into the pot and took a taste.

Wrinkling his nose, he turned to Lizzie and asked, "This isn't cheese, is it?"

"It's candle wax," said Lizzie.

Matt cracked up, slapping his hand on the kitchen table as he laughed. Until his parents glanced at him. Then he stood up straight, put on a serious face, and left the room.

The next day at school, Lizzie and Miranda made their way through the cafeteria line. Trying to fill their plates with whatever looked edible was always a challenge, but they managed to find some French fries, the always present U.F.S. (Unidentifiable Fried Stuff), and pepperoni pizza.

With her mind on their latest homework assignment, Miranda said, "I think the perfect town would be five hundred Hot Topic stores and a ten-story shopping mall."

Lizzie looked down at the sheet their

teacher had passed out and read from it. "Design a model community, including housing, hospitals, schools, and police and fire departments."

"Police and fire departments," Miranda said in a singsong voice, making fun of their teacher.

Lizzie joined in, bobbing her head from left to right as she said, "Housing, hospitals, and schools."

"We'll call it Boringville, U.S.A.," Miranda said, sitting down at their usual table. "Where do they come up with these moronic assignments?"

"The Moronic Assignment Study Guide," Lizzie explained. "It's like this thick," she said, holding her hand three feet from the ground.

As Gordo approached, he asked, "Lemme guess—that's how tall Tom Cruise is."

"Tom Cruise isn't short," Miranda said, defending the actor, who she thought was a total hottie. "He just has small bones."

"Okay, Gordo, imagine you live in a boring suburb where all the houses look alike and everybody's predictable," said Lizzie.

"I do live in a boring suburb where all the houses look alike and everyone's predictable," Gordo replied. "Thank you."

"Okay," Lizzie said. "But if you could pick any businesses you want on Main Street, what would they be?"

Gordo didn't have to think twice. Pausing with his plastic fork in midair, he said, "A bookstore containing the works of Navajo and Greek philosophers, a coffeehouse where people only discuss music and politics, a thousand-foot water slide ending in a swim-up counter where they serve free, deep-fried pizza. And Tyra Banks would be the mayor.

I've given this a lot of thought." He stabbed his fork into a piece of U.F.S.

No kidding, thought Lizzie.

Just then, Kate Sanders walked up to their table, ignoring Lizzie, which was only slightly better than sneering at her. She asked, "Hey, Gordo, do you know where the nearest Software Shack is?"

"Yeah, it's over on Collins Street," Gordo answered.

Kate tossed her long, perfect blond hair over one shoulder. "Would they have that software that designs cities and towns and stuff?"

"You mean Cyber Townmaker?" asked Gordo. "They should."

Lizzie blinked at Kate. Her former best friend wasn't just the Queen of Mean—she was the entire Royal Court. "Okay, Kate. We're supposed to do this assignment ourselves."

"Whatever," Kate replied with a sneer.

"You're supposed to use your imagination, not have some computer do it for you," said Lizzie. Then she turned to Gordo, obviously irritated, and said, "Gordo, why didn't you tell me there was a program like that?"

"Well, it costs sixty bucks," he answered.

He turned to Kate. "I don't think you can afford it," he told her.

"Hello," said Kate. "I baby-sat *twice* last week."

Kate could baby-sit? This was so unfair! Lizzie knew she could do such a better job than the snob. What did Kate know about baby-sitting? Sure, Lizzie thought, baby-sitting was probably a snap for Kate—once she learned how to tune out the crying and whining kids. Kate probably thought it was all about getting paid to talk on the phone, polish her nails, and eat whatever great food she could find in the refrigerator. Ugh!

Pulling a wad of cash from her wallet, Kate began to count out the bills. "Twenty, forty, sixty . . . Oh, look, I have more." After waving her cash in the air, and making sure Lizzie, Miranda, and Gordo were adequately awed, she walked away.

Lizzie watched her go. "Kate baby-sits?" she said. "Since when does Kate baby-sit? Why don't they just make her Queen of the World and be done with it?"

"Baby-sitting sounds like a pretty sweet gig. Why don't you do it?" asked Gordo.

Lizzie winced. "I don't baby-sit. I get baby-sat." Lizzie imagined herself trapped in a playpen, with some chubby-cheeked elderly woman shoving a stuffed bunny rabbit in her face. The thought made her want to hide under a rock, as far away from Kate Sanders and everyone else as she could get.

"I don't get it," she said. "I mean, I'm the same age as Kate. I'm as mature as she is. I'm responsible. . . ."

Later that day Lizzie pleaded with her parents. ". . . and I want to baby-sit!"

"Absolutely not," said Mr. McGuire as he sat at the kitchen table, touching up the paint job on a lawn gnome.

Lizzie was so upset, she almost stamped her foot. Of course, she realized that throwing a tantrum like a kid was not the best way to prove she was mature enough to take *care* of kids. "But Kate Sanders baby-sits."

"She does?" Mrs. McGuire asked, wondering for a second if she could see if Kate was free on Saturday.

Mr. McGuire, doing that mind-reading thing that Lizzie's parents can do with each other, shook his head *no*. So Mrs. McGuire shifted her tone of voice to neutral. "I mean, she, she does, huh?"

"Yes," Lizzie told them. "And you haven't found a sitter for tonight. And you trust me to ride the bus to school all by myself. Why can't you trust me to baby-sit?"

"Hmmm." As Mrs. McGuire carried a stack of plates and silverware from the island to the kitchen table, she tried to come up with a reason. When none came to mind, she realized Lizzie might be on to something.

i think i'm getting a nibble here.

Mrs. McGuire turned to her husband. "Maybe she has a point."

"And Miranda can help me. She watches her baby sister after school," Lizzie said. She didn't mention the fact that Miranda always complained about how gross it was to have to change her sister's dirty, smelly diapers.

Still, Mr. McGuire didn't budge. "Sweetheart, you're just not ready yet. This is a big responsibility."

"Well, you've always told me I can do anything if I set my mind to it," Lizzie said. "And I've set my mind to this. I can do it."

"We do say that, Sam," Mrs. McGuire had to admit to Mr. McGuire.

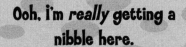 

Ooh, I'm *really* getting a nibble here.

Mr. McGuire panicked. "But Matt can be quite a handful," he tried.

Mrs. McGuire turned toward the living room, where Matt was lying facedown on the couch. You might think he was asleep, except whenever a commercial came on—then he managed to point the remote at the TV and change the channel. "Matt, what would you do if Lizzie baby-sat you?"

"I dunno," Matt replied lazily, not taking his eyes off his cartoons. "Watch TV, I guess."

"Thank you for the help, pal," Mr. McGuire quipped, sarcastically. He turned back to his lawn gnome and tried to paint, but he knew Lizzie was waiting for an answer. "All right. Maybe we can give this a try."

Yes! Lizzie was so psyched! "Thanks, Dad." She gave her father a gigantic hug. "It means a lot to me that you can trust me. I'll do a great job."

CHAPTER TWO

That night, Matt sat on the sofa, playing a video game and eating popcorn. Lizzie and Miranda were on the floor, arranging empty cereal boxes and juice containers for their model community. They even had an electric train set chugging around town in a loop. By offering good public transportation, Lizzie planned to create a more environmentally friendly city, where people didn't need to depend on cars.

"Okay," Lizzie said. "The Coco Drops will be city hall."

Miranda grabbed a handful of the cereal and ate some. "I just ate the mayor," she said.

Just then, Mr. and Mrs. McGuire came downstairs, all dressed up for their big date. Mr. McGuire's conservative dark suit didn't go so well with the freaked-out look on his face. "Lizzie," he said. "I added some numbers to the emergency phone list. Also, I moved all the cleaners out from under the kitchen sink. And whatever you do, do not open the door for anybody."

"And I won't follow the trail of bread crumbs to the gingerbread witch's house," Lizzie said. "Dad, don't worry."

Mr. McGuire exhaled, loudly. He couldn't even pretend that he wasn't nervous. His heart was racing, his palms were sweating, and his feet felt like they were glued to the floor.

He would have done anything to stay at home, but Mrs. McGuire had insisted they go out.

The doorbell rang and Mrs. McGuire answered it. "Hey, Gordo," she said.

"Hi, Mrs. McGuire." Gordo slipped into the house. "My parents said I could come over if that's okay with you."

"Oh, sure," said Mrs. McGuire. "But Lizzie and Miranda are baby-sitting Matt, so I don't know how much fun you're gonna have."

"Oh, I know. I'm not about fun. I'm about the green," said Gordo.

Mrs. McGuire was thoroughly confused and turned to her daughter for a translation. "Lizzie?"

"Money," Lizzie answered.

Sinking down on the couch, Gordo grabbed a bowl of popcorn from Miranda's lap. "I'm gonna earn my money indoors," he said. "Sitting on a sofa, eating someone else's popcorn."

"Hey, that's mine." Miranda grabbed for the bowl, but Gordo held it out of her reach.

"Lizzie, Matt's bedtime is nine o'clock," Mr. McGuire said.

"Yes, Dad, I know." Lizzie stood up and pushed her parents toward the front door. "Dad, listen, everything's under control. I've got it all handled, okay?"

Mr. McGuire said, "Okay, now both our cell phones are charged. And we're trusting you, Lizzie."

"Whoa," said Lizzie. "Can I hear that again?"

"Both of our cell phones are charged?" he asked.

"No, no, no," said Lizzie. "The other part."

"We're trusting you," Mr. McGuire repeated.

"Yeah, that," Lizzie said, happily.

Ta-da! After all these years—trust!

"Thanks, Dad." Lizzie watched her parents leave, thinking, I'm alone in the house, with trust—this is way cool.

Wow. For the first time in my life, I'm in charge. I'm the ranking adult in the house. I'm Queen of the World!

"Alone, at last," Lizzie mused.

"I don't see why you have to muscle in on baby-sitting, Gordo. This is how *we* make money," Miranda complained.

"Why should girls have a monopoly on baby-sitting?" Gordo asked.

"Because boys have a monopoly on burping the Pledge of Allegiance," Miranda answered. "We deserve some kind of monopoly."

"Hey, I love that game," said Matt. "I wanna be the race car."

"Tough luck," Lizzie told him. "You're gonna watch *Willie Wonka*."

"I've seen that ten times," Matt protested. "I wanna be the race car!"

"Well, we've got homework," said Lizzie. "If you'll be patient, we'll maybe play later, okay?"

"All right." Matt sighed.

Lizzie smiled at her friends. She handled that well. She and Gordo high-fived, and Lizzie realized that this baby-sitting thing was a piece of cake—with extra chocolate frosting on top!

Two minutes later, Matt was jumping up and down on the sofa, like he was the Energizer bunny on overload. "Race car! Race car! Race car! Race car! Race car!" He chanted as he bounced so hard and fast that Lizzie couldn't believe the couch springs didn't pop right through the fabric.

Lizzie's, Gordo's, and Miranda's heads moved up and down as they watched Matt bouncing. It was like they were keeping their eyes on a ball in some kind of weird, vertical Ping-Pong tournament.

"Anyone got any ideas?" Lizzie asked.

Miranda and Gordo shook their heads.

"Sorry," Miranda said.

"I got nothing," Gordo added.

Matt jumped off the couch and zipped around the room. "Race car! Race car!" he shouted, leaping back onto the couch. It was almost as bad as the maple syrup night!

Meanwhile Mr. and Mrs. McGuire arrived at Panda Garden, their favorite Chinese restaurant. The hostess, Mrs. Shin, greeted them with a warm smile and showed them to their table. "Here you go, Mr. and Mrs. McGuire. Your regular table."

"Thank you, Mrs. Shin." Mr. McGuire settled down into his seat.

"Haven't seen you since the Year of the Tiger," said Mrs. Shin.

"Yeah, well, it's really hard to get a reliable baby-sitter," Mr. McGuire explained.

"Well, glad to have you back," Mrs. Shin said. "I'll be back with some wontons."

Mrs. McGuire smiled and said, "Thank you."

Mr. McGuire picked up one corner of his bright orange napkin and unfolded it. He tried not to think of what was going on back at the house, but a list of possible disasters ran through his mind: fires and floods, break-ins and broken limbs. . . . He strained to listen for fire, ambulance, or police sirens outside.

Mrs. McGuire said, "Sam, would you please relax. It's one night out. Lizzie can handle it. I mean that. Everything's gonna be fine."

Mr. McGuire picked up his wooden chopsticks, which were joined at the top, separated them, and started rubbing them together to get rid of any splinters.

Back at the McGuire house, Lizzie was on her hands and knees, furiously scrubbing at a new purple stain on the rug. Matt dabbed at a second, matching purple stain on his shirt.

"This had better come out of the carpet, Matt," said Lizzie, annoyed that the more she tried to clean, the bigger the stain became.

She glared at Miranda. "What did you give him grape juice for? I told you ginger ale. Ginger ale isn't purple."

"Grape juice was the only thing that would shut him up," said Miranda. "He won't do a thing you say."

"Matt, go upstairs," Lizzie said. "Change your shirt and get cleaned up. Now."

"No," Matt said, simply.

"See?" Miranda said. She wanted to say, "I told you so," but knew it would upset Lizzie too much. Baby-sitting her sister was *never* this hard. Of course, Miranda's little sister was still too young to talk back.

"Zip it," Lizzie said to Miranda.

"Why should I? *He* won't," Miranda pointed out, oh-so-helpfully.

Lizzie was feeling desperate. "Matt, starting right now, you do everything I tell you, or I'll tell Mom and Dad."

"Nuh-uh," Matt said with a satisfied little grin. "You want Mom and Dad to think you're a good baby-sitter, so you're gonna say things went great."

"Then I'll squash you like a bug instead," Lizzie said.

"Then I'll tell Mom and Dad." Matt sat down on the couch and made himself comfortable. He had his sister just where he wanted her! "Face it—I'm in charge here."

Lizzie raised her voice. "No, *I* am in charge here."

Gordo stepped in and said, "Matt, what do you say we go upstairs and find you a clean shirt?"

"Okay," Matt said.

"How come he does what you say?" Lizzie asked, totally outraged.

"I'm an older man," Gordo explained. "He's impressed by me."

"Well, I'm in charge here, and he's supposed to do what *I* say, not what you say," Lizzie replied.

"Who cares who says to do it?" Gordo asked. "He needs a new shirt. He's as sticky as the floor of a movie theater."

Lizzie was about to protest when she saw Matt inching dangerously close to the wall. "Matt, don't lean there!" she said. Too late.

Matt tried to move away from the wall, but couldn't. "I'm stuck," he said.

"Matt?" Lizzie grabbed onto one of Matt's arms and pulled. She was horrified to discover that he was, in fact, stuck to the wall like a gnat to flypaper.

CHAPTER THREE

Whoever said that tea was supposed to calm your nerves never met a man who just let his daughter baby-sit for the first time. Mr. McGuire took a sip from his small cup of tea. Nope, not relaxing at all. Not one bit. He wondered what was going on back at the house, and if he had remembered to lock all the doors, and to tell Lizzie and Matt not to play with matches.

"Gosh, it is so nice to eat out, just the two of us for a change," Mrs. McGuire said, calmly.

"Yep, nice." Mr. McGuire rubbed his chopsticks together, not realizing he'd been doing just that for the past ten minutes.

"Sam, you're turning your chopsticks into toothpicks. Want to settle down? You're fidgeting," Mrs. McGuire observed.

"No, I'm not," said Mr. McGuire, as he fidgeted away.

Mrs. McGuire shot him a look that asked, "Who are you trying to fool?"

"Okay, look," said Mr. McGuire. "I just think it was a mistake leaving Lizzie in charge."

Mrs. McGuire said, "But she never gets in trouble at school. She gets there and back all by herself, and she's the only one in the house who knows how to make the picture-in-picture work."

"Yeah, but she sleeps until noon on the weekends. She uses the picture-in-picture to watch MTV and cartoons at the same time." When his wife didn't say anything Mr. McGuire started to stand up. "I gotta go check on her."

"No, you do not," Mrs. McGuire said, in her sternest voice that was usually reserved for talking to Matt and Lizzie. "Do you know how much it meant to her that you trusted her?"

"Okay, I tell you what," Mr. McGuire said. "I'll just sneak in, look in a window. She'll never even know I'm there."

Mrs. McGuire sighed. "Okay. If I let you go, do you promise me that you will come right back here and eat your meal in peace?"

"Yeah." Mr. McGuire nodded, flashing his wife a grin.

"Okay," Mrs. McGuire said with a sigh.

As Mr. McGuire bolted up out of his seat and ran for the front door, Mrs. McGuire said, "But she'd better not know you're there. I swear she will never forgive you."

"Okay," Mr. McGuire called, already halfway out the door.

"And I won't forgive you until she does," Mrs. McGuire added.

Lizzie scrubbed furiously at the grape juice stain. Matt's old shirt was stuck to the wall, but at least he'd gone upstairs to change into a clean one.

Hearing a strange buzzing noise, Lizzie looked up to see Matt with the vacuum cleaner. The day's newspaper was stuck to the hose. "Look, it holds up newspapers," he said.

"Cut it out, Matt," Lizzie said.

Ignoring her, Matt looked for something else to suction. He came back a minute later. "Look, it holds up Mom's cat calendar."

"Gordo, can you tell him to quit that?" Lizzie yelled.

"You're in charge—you do it," Gordo said, not taking his eyes off the television.

"Could you at least help?" Lizzie cried. "You didn't come over here to watch TV on the couch."

Realizing that Lizzie had a good point, Gordo stood up and turned the TV off. "All right," he said. "I'll watch TV in your room."

"Miranda, get me more paper towels," Lizzie said.

"Pass," Miranda replied. "I'm building a ten-story shopping mall for Mirandaville."

"Well, Mirandaville doesn't need a ten-story shopping mall," said Lizzie, somewhat hysterically. "We need a hospital."

"Fine." Miranda shrugged. "I'll go drink some orange juice and make a mall out of that!"

"Fine! Nobody help me do anything!" Lizzie yelled.

Matt walked over to Lizzie with the vacuum. "Look, it holds up Dad's briefcase."

"I'll just handle everything myself!" Lizzie yelled.

Suddenly, the vacuum motor made a funny noise and burned out. Half a second later, all of the electricity cut out, plunging everyone into darkness.

"Um, I may need a little help here," said Lizzie, looking around the room.

i hate it when Dad's right.

Matt found a flashlight, held it up to his chin, and turned it on. With only his face lit up he said in a voice trembling with fear, "Lizzie, I'm scared!" A second later, he said in a deep and scratchy voice, "Look at me, I'm a monster." Next he whispered, "I see dead people."

"Cut it out, Matt," Lizzie warned.

Meanwhile, Mr. McGuire crept up to the house slowly, feeling like a burglar from an old movie. Since all the curtains were drawn, he couldn't see inside. And because they were so thick, he couldn't see that the lights were off. But looking up, he noticed the transom over the door. A clear window! If only it weren't so high up . . .

In the kitchen, Lizzie lit some of her new candles.

"Whew, that stinks!" Matt said, holding his nose in disgust.

"It's vanilla," Lizzie said, through clenched teeth. "It's soothing."

Miranda raised her eyebrows. "Works like a charm," she said, sarcastically.

Gordo walked into the kitchen and waved his hand in front of his face. "Whoa! Who's burning garbage?"

"I'm trying to get some light in here," Lizzie said. "If you're not going to help me, you could at least hush up."

"Don't tell us to 'hush up,'" Miranda said. "We're not babies."

"You're *acting* like babies," Lizzie replied.

"It's a shame there isn't a decent baby-sitter around," Gordo said.

Ouch! Lizzie looked around the house. She took in the stained rug, the shorted-out electricity, and Matt's sticky shirt. "I'm sure there'll be a decent baby-sitter around next time," she said. "'Cause I obviously can't handle it."

* * *

Back outside, Mr. McGuire climbed onto the seat of a chair, and tried to peek in the window, but found he still wasn't tall enough. He stepped to the back of the chair, and tried to pull his body up with his fingertips. He was almost there, when the chair gave out from under him, and he tumbled to the ground, slamming his neck into the pointy little hat of the lawn gnome. "Ahh!" he shouted.

Lizzie jumped up and aimed her flashlight toward the back door. "What was that?"

"Do you think it's a burglar?" asked Miranda.

"Naw," said Gordo. "It's probably just a raccoon. They root around in the trash and stuff."

"Yeah, it's probably just a raccoon. Let's make noises, just in case," said Lizzie.

She rang a bell as Miranda belted out the

only tune she could think of: "My country 'tis of thee, sweet land of liberty, of thee I sing." She was way off-key, and if anything was going to spook a burglar, her singing was *so* it.

"I'm gonna go and flip the circuit breakers, so we can play some loud music," said Gordo. Glancing at Miranda, he added, "Real music."

Mr. McGuire sat on the ground, coughing and rubbing his neck, which seriously ached. As he tried to remember what had happened, his cell phone began to ring. "Hello?" he croaked.

"What is taking so long?" asked Mrs. McGuire. She was still at Panda Garden, staring at the tableful of delicious but now cold food.

"All the curtains are shut," Mr. McGuire explained hoarsely, between coughs. "And I can't see in the house."

"Okay, just get in there, pretend you forgot your wallet, make sure they're okay, and get right out," said Mrs. McGuire.

"Gotcha."

"What's wrong with your voice?"

"Uh, mmm, lawn gnome," Mr. McGuire replied. As soon as he hung up, the lights in the house went on.

Miranda turned on the stereo, blasting pop music. Lizzie stopped ringing her bell as Gordo entered the room.

"You think it went away, right?" she asked.

"A raccoon wouldn't stick around through this racket," Gordo said.

Suddenly, the doorknob started to turn. The door slowly creaked open, but only by a couple of inches, since the chain was fastened.

Lizzie screamed.

"A raccoon wouldn't do that, either," Miranda observed.

"Kids, open up—it's me," Mr. McGuire croaked.

Code Blue! Seeing the outline of a man's body and an actual hand groping around inside, Lizzie shouted, "It *is* a burglar!" She ran to her little brother and gave him a hug. "Matt!"

"Lizzie!" Matt exclaimed, truly scared.

Meanwhile, Mr. McGuire forced his hand further through the crack in the door and tried to unlatch the chain.

Lizzie knew she had to do something. She was the baby-sitter, after all. Everyone's safety depended on her. Taking a deep breath, she yelled, "AAAGGHH!" and charged at the door. Lizzie slammed into it with all her might, crushing what she thought was a stranger's wrist.

Crunch! A searing pain shot up Mr. McGuire's arm and he screamed in agony. "Aarrgh!" He pulled his hand free and checked for damage.

Meanwhile, Lizzie stood with her back pressed against the door.

"That ought to drive him away," said Gordo.

Matt clung to his sister. "Lizzie, I'm really scared."

"It's okay. I'm not gonna let anything happen to you, okay?" said Lizzie. "We're gonna call the police."

Matt's and Lizzie's frightened eyes locked. Lizzie thought, You may be an annoying twerp with hair that looks like the back of a porcupine, but you're still my brother. Matt thought, Although you're totally bossy and you finished all the Froot Loops last week, you're really not so bad.

* * *

Meanwhile, Mr. McGuire was stumbling around outside. Water! he thought. Water will soothe my aching pain. He plunged his hand into the kiddie pool, breathed in deeply, and tried to come up with a new plan to break into his own house.

CHAPTER FOUR

Back at Panda Garden, Mrs. Shin sat next to Mrs. McGuire and they both stared at the tableful of delicious, untouched food.

"You know," said Mrs. Shin, "I have a cousin. Knows how to treat a lady."

"Mrs. Shin, my husband didn't leave me," said Mrs. McGuire. "I mean, he left me but he didn't leave me."

Mrs. Shin shook her head. "Aw, yeah, you're keeping your chin up." She shoveled some steamed dumplings onto Mrs. McGuire's plate. "Brave, brave, little soldier girl."

Mr. McGuire shook his hand dry, pulled out his cell phone, and dialed the house.

Lizzie picked up on the first ring. "Hello?"

"It's me," her dad croaked into the phone with his hoarse voice.

Lizzie's eyes widened in terror. "It's him!"

"I'm at home!" Mr. McGuire tried to explain.

But Lizzie misheard him. "He knows we're alone!" she cried.

Mr. McGuire dragged his injured body to the door. "Come on, kids," he said as he jiggled the doorknob one more time.

Lizzie screamed, and then Miranda, Gordo, and Matt joined her.

Matt even slapped his hands to his cheeks and struck a perfect *Home Alone* pose.

"It's worse!" said Miranda in a shaking voice. "He's at the door."

"Gordo, Miranda, get the train-transformer," Lizzie said, thinking fast.

Mr. McGuire continued to shake the knob and pound on the door.

Back inside, Gordo wrapped the lead wires from the Mirandaville train set around the doorknob. When everything was secure, he signaled to Lizzie, who kneeled by a power outlet with the transformer cord in her hand.

"Now!" said Gordo.

It was action time! As Lizzie plugged the cord in, Matt flipped the lever and sparks leaped from the doorknob.

Mr. McGuire, who was holding the door-knob, received a huge jolt of juice. He shook all over and tried to let go, but it felt like his hand was superglued to the door. He was finally able to pull away from the evil grip of the doorknob. But like a tug-of-war where the other team lets go of the rope midgame, he flew backward, tripped over the gnome, and landed right in the kiddie pool.

"Lawn gnome," he moaned indignantly.

Back at the McGuire house, everyone was still in a state of panic. They raced around, checking the doors and windows to make sure everything was secure.

Mr. McGuire knew none of this, and he'd had enough. He found his hacksaw in the garage and limped back toward the door.

As Matt and Lizzie double-locked the French doors in back, Matt said, "You can baby-sit for me anytime."

"Let's get through tonight first, okay?" Lizzie responded.

Suddenly, she heard a sawing sound. Looking toward the back door, she saw the top half of the hacksaw moving back and forth, eating its way through the chain.

Lizzie screamed. Then she came up with a plan. "Gordo, get the train. Miranda, fill the paint can with flour, now!" To Matt she shouted, "Come on, come on!"

Mr. McGuire sawed away, pleased that he was actually making progress.

Miranda looped a long piece of twine through the handle of the paint can full of flour, as Gordo lashed a paring knife to the swinging arm of the crossing gate. Once Matt wolfed down a grape Popsicle, Lizzie took the stick and taped it to the train transformer lever, and placed it by the door. Lizzie and her friends assembled these various parts into the perfect booby trap! They weren't going to let this maniac get into the house without pounding him hard!

* * *

The intruder was still working the lock, and laughing maniacally with frustration. Lizzie darted into the kitchen, to join everyone else who was hiding behind the counter.

"That was some fast Popsicle eating, Matt," Lizzie said.

Matt's mouth was ringed with purple. "Thanks," he said, raising his fingers to his forehead. "I have major brain-freeze."

Once Mr. McGuire cut through the chain, he turned the doorknob, thinking, Victory, finally!

As the door opened, the Popsicle stick pushed the train transformer to full speed.

The locomotive sped across the kitchen floor with a long piece of twine tied to it. The twine was threaded through a hook in the ceiling, and the other end was fastened to a paint can. . . . And as the train chugged down the track, it pulled the paint can higher and higher!

Then, suddenly . . .

"Dad?" asked Matt, surprised that the burglar was his own father.

But before Matt could stop it, the train reached the end of the track, where a knife attached to the crossing gate arm swung down. The twine was severed in an instant. It released the paint can, which came swinging down from the ceiling to hit Mr. McGuire in the stomach!

"Youch!" he yelped as he doubled over and was sent flying back outside.

Lizzie, Matt, Gordo, and Miranda watched from behind the counter, completely stunned.

"You guys have to trust me," said Gordo. "You have no idea how much that hurts."

"Omigosh! Your poor father," said Miranda.

They walked across the kitchen and peeked out into the backyard, where Mr. McGuire was writhing in pain. He kicked the lawn gnome hard, smashing his toe in the process. Angry, in pain, feeling pathetic, and soaked to the bone, he jumped around.

Matt leaned against the door frame and said, "We are so in trouble."

"He was supposed to trust me," Lizzie said, in a hurt voice.

"Well," Gordo said. "If he was spying on you—and I admit it does look like he was—I'd think he suffered enough."

Just then, a police car with flashing red lights pulled into the driveway. A police siren blasted, and then a voice came over the loud-speaker: "Sir, please put your hands on your head and don't move."

Moments later, two cops led the intruder to the house. "I'm telling you, I live here," he was saying. "My kids are inside."

Unsure of whether or not to believe this wet and clearly disturbed man, one of the officers knocked on the door.

Mr. McGuire explained, "I just came home to check on them."

Lizzie opened the door, wearing her best "I'm innocent, didn't do it, don't know what's going on" expression. "Yes?" she asked.

"Hello, young lady," said the policeman. "Is this man your father?"

Lizzie blinked and refused to even look at her dad when she said, "I don't know why my father would be sneaking around in the bushes late at night. Maybe that means he doesn't trust me." She shrugged one shoulder, innocently.

"Lizzie!" Mr. McGuire muttered through clenched teeth.

Lizzie rolled her eyes to the sky. "That's my father," she told the officers.

"Good night, sir," said one cop. "And by the way, your lawn gnome is broken."

Later that night, wrapped in a bright blue towel, Mr. McGuire slumped over the kitchen counter. Mrs. McGuire rubbed his back.

"You were supposed to trust me," Lizzie reminded her dad.

Mrs. McGuire nodded. "Yes, we were. And we didn't stick to our word, and we were wrong."

They're admitting they were wrong? Call the news crews. Film at eleven.

Mr. McGuire sat up and tried to explain

himself. "It's not that I don't trust you, sweet-heart. I guess I still just think of you as the six-year-old girl that used to need me to chase the monsters out of her closet. I guess I have to get used to the fact that you're not that little girl anymore. You're becoming a young lady, and I have to let you act like one."

Lizzie's anger melted away with each word of her dad's sappy-but-sweet explanation. Hmm, now how can I milk this? she wondered. "So, I can go on a real date?" she asked.

"No," said Mr. McGuire.

"Will you teach me how to drive?" she tried.

"No," said Mr. McGuire.

"Can I dye my hair?"

No, again.

"Well, what can I do?" she asked.

"You can baby-sit Matt next Saturday night," Mrs. McGuire said.

"Yeah," said Mr. McGuire, knowing that next time he'd stay far away from the house when Lizzie was in charge. He had a feeling he'd be sorry if he didn't!

So, the more responsibility i ask for, the more responsibility i get stuck with. That stinks. i think.

Okay, it wasn't as good as driving, or dating, or dyeing her hair, but baby-sitting was *something*. And it felt pretty great.

Don't close the book on Lizzie yet!
Here's a sneak peek at the next
Lizzie McGuire story. . . .

Adapted by Jasmine Jones
Based on the series created by Terri Minsky
Based on a teleplay written
by Melissa Gould

"**O**kay," Lizzie said as she held up a tube of
lilac-colored lip gloss. "This one says berry,
but it tastes so much like vanilla. I love it,
anyway. Here—try it, Miranda."

Lizzie reached across Gordo, who was propped up at the Digital Bean counter, reading a monster truck magazine, and handed the gloss to Miranda, who frowned at it, then unscrewed the top and gave it a sniff.

"Look, the Monster Truck Roundup is coming to town!" Gordo said in a voice that was unnaturally excited, given that he was talking about big, loud cars. Gordo was generally more of a small, gas-efficient-car kind of guy. "Six fun-filled hours of monster truck force and monster truck action!"

Lizzie looked at Gordo. What was his deal with monster trucks all of a sudden? Usually, the only monsters Gordo was interested in were the ones in 1950s-era black-and-white films—and that was only for artistic wisecrack-making purposes.

"What?" Gordo demanded. "I'm sick of talking about girl stuff." He scowled over at Miranda, who was busy applying the berry-vanilla lip gloss and smacking her lips.

"Gordo, lip gloss is important," Lizzie protested. "By the way, since when have you been interested in monster trucks?"

"I'm a guy," Gordo said defensively. "And, we never talk about guy stuff."

Lizzie looked over at Miranda, who was completely lost in Lip Gloss World. "Miranda?" Lizzie called.

Miranda snapped out of it and smiled over at Lizzie. "Oh! Hi," she said, joining the conversation.

Gordo frowned. "Are you okay?"

"Yeah, you've been kind of quiet," Lizzie agreed.

Miranda shook her head. "I don't know what's wrong with me. I can't eat. I can't sleep. I've been, like, totally distracted."

"Why?"

Miranda's eyebrows drew together. "I don't know. It all started in drama class yesterday when Ryan Adams did that monologue."

"Oh, yeah." Gordo nodded, remembering. "He was pretty good."

Miranda grimaced and shot Gordo the Look of Death. "Good?" she demanded. "*Good?* Ryan Adams wasn't good! He was *amazing*, Gordo." She rolled her eyes to the ceiling and sighed. "Amazing!"

Lizzie thought back to drama class. Which one was Ryan again? Oh, yeah. He was that tall kid who did some weird monologue where he had to talk to himself, saying all this totally bizarr-o stuff about "To be or not to be." Lizzie guessed it had been okay. She had been kind of distracted by this hangnail that had been bothering her all day.

"And wasn't he cute, Lizzie?" Miranda gushed. "And smart. Really smart. And . . .

what's that word?" Miranda wracked her brain. "Charismatic?" she guessed, then nodded. "He looked charismatic. I thought he was amazing, funny, and smart."

Lizzie grinned at her friend. "Oh my gosh," she said suddenly. "This is so exciting, Miranda!"

"I know!" Gordo agreed enthusiastically as he buried his nose back into his monster truck magazine. Where did that thing come from, anyway? Lizzie wondered. "Nothing says 'exciting' like the Monster Truck Roundup," Gordo added.

"Not that!" Lizzie protested. She pointed to where Miranda was grinning like a Cheshire cat in a pile of catnip. "This!"

She loves him, she loves him not, she loves him. She loves him not. She loves him, she loves him, she loves him!

"What?" Miranda asked.

"Miranda," Lizzie explained, "you're in love!" She nearly laughed out loud—it was so obvious! How could Miranda not see it?

Miranda looked completely confused. "I am?"

Gordo stared at Lizzie. "With who?"

Lizzie rolled her eyes. "With Ryan!" Sheesh, Lizzie thought. Am I the only one paying attention here?

Miranda touched her hair self-consciously. "Really?"

"She doesn't even know him!" Gordo protested.

"Yes, I do!" Miranda insisted. "Didn't you hear that monologue? He was sensitive, he was cute, he was funny—"

"All right, all right, enough." Gordo flipped closed his magazine and hauled himself off his stool. "I've got to start hanging out with some guys," he said, shaking his head. Gordo waved his hand dismissively in Lizzie's general direction and wandered out of the Digital Bean.

Miranda watched him go for a minute, scooted over, and took the seat Gordo had just left. "So, what do we do now?"

"Listen," Lizzie said, "as your friend, I'm going to do everything I can to get you two together."

What am i saying? i have no idea what to do.

Lizzie looked into Miranda's glowing eyes and gulped. Okay, she thought, I just promised to help make Ryan Adams her boyfriend, and I have no clue how to do it.

Then again, Lizzie mused, that's never really stopped me before.

Sure, she thought, I can do this. After all, how hard can it be?

The next morning, Lizzie walked up to the counter in the kitchen where her annoying little brother, Matt, was already chowing down on a bowl of cereal. Lizzie reached for the box, and shook some of the wholesome wheat nuggets her mom had bought into her bowl. Lizzie frowned at the cereal, wondering why Mrs. McGuire wouldn't let her family have a box of Sugar-O's, like normal people.

Just as Lizzie lifted her spoon, she caught a movement out of the corner of her eye. She looked over to where Matt was making a face that was even uglier than his usual one.

"Mom!" Lizzie called. "Matt's staring at me."

Mrs. McGuire didn't even look up from the

Rolodex she was flipping through. "Matt, stop staring at your sister," she said automatically.

Lizzie took another spoonful of cereal, but now Matt was making puking motions . . . and sound effects to go with them.

"What are you doing?" Mrs. McGuire demanded, looking at Matt.

"Clearing my throat," Matt said innocently. Then he launched into another round of vomit noises.

"Oh, Matt," Mrs. McGuire said, warningly.

Lizzie rolled her eyes. Did her mother seriously think that her I'm-So-Disappointed-in-You-Voice was going to have any effect? Didn't she realize that only worked on Lizzie?

Mr. McGuire walked into the kitchen. "Morning, kids."

"Morning, Dad," Matt said brightly.

"Dad," Lizzie complained, "Matt won't let me eat my breakfast."

"Matt, let your sister eat her breakfast," Mr. McGuire said semi-sternly.

"But her face hurts," Matt protested.

"What?" Mr. McGuire looked over at Lizzie, worried.

Lizzie scowled at Matt. "What? My face doesn't hurt."

"I thought it did," Matt said seriously, then broke into a grin, "because it's killing me." He slapped the kitchen island and roared at his own joke.

Mrs. McGuire turned to her husband. "It's been going on all morning," she explained.

"All morning?" Mr. McGuire repeated. "Try 'their whole lives.'"

Lizzie narrowed her eyes at Matt. "What are you eating for breakfast?" she demanded. "A big bowl of ugly?" She shoved her cereal away and hopped off her stool. "I'm going to school."

"Ooh, I'll miss you," Matt said, batting his eyes at Lizzie. Then he rolled his eyes and snorted. "Not."

"Come on, you two," Mr. McGuire protested. "We're a family. We're supposed to like each other."

"But I *do* like Matt," Lizzie insisted. "I like it when he's not around. Later," she said as she stalked out of the kitchen.

Seriously, Lizzie thought as she grabbed her book bag, that's the best thing about school— I get to escape from Matt for six whole hours. Compared to hanging out with my little brother, school looks like an island paradise. Especially now that I've got this cool new project to work on—the Miranda Love Project!

I'm going for an A-plus.

"Ryan is totally the guy for me," Miranda said, breathlessly, as she and Lizzie stood in front of their lockers. "You're so smart to figure that out, Lizzie.

Flattery goes a long way.

"I mean, he's sensitive, he's funny. . . ." Miranda went on. "I mean, you could tell by the way he played that part, don't you think? I can't wait to tell him how good he was."

"Yeah," Lizzie agreed. "I'm sure he'll appreciate it."

"So, how do I look?" Miranda asked, fiddling with her multicolored crocheted cap. "He should be walking by any minute. I usually see him between classes."

"Yeah, you look great," Lizzie said encouragingly. Then she bit her lip and added, "Except that you're sweating a little bit."

"I am?" Miranda asked in a panicky voice. "Where?"

Lizzie gestured to Miranda's locker.

"Oh, right," Miranda said quickly. She yanked the locker door open so she could look at herself in her mirror. Unfortunately, she opened it too fast and ended up whacking Lizzie in the face.

"Ow!" Lizzie stumbled backward and slid to the floor in a heap.

Buh-bye.

"Lizzie," Miranda cried, looking down at her friend. "Are you okay?"

Lizzie nodded deliriously. Am I okay? she wondered. Well, except for the massive pain in my forehead and the horrible dizziness, I think I'm doing great. She held out her hand. "Oh, yeah, yeah, just help me up?"

Miranda reached for Lizzie's hand. "Sure."

"Ooh, there's Ryan!" Lizzie whispered fiercely as Miranda helped her struggle to her feet.

Miranda turned to look . . . and dropped Lizzie.

"Ow," Lizzie said as she dropped to the floor. *Again*, she added mentally.

But Miranda wasn't paying attention . . . she was on a mission. She stepped right in front of Ryan.

He smiled at her, a little uncertainly. "Hi," he said.

"Hi," Miranda said brightly. "Hi." Her mouth kept moving, and sounds were coming out, but they weren't making much sense. "I um . . . um . . . um . . ."

Lizzie stared at Miranda. What was going on? It wasn't like Miranda to get nervous around a guy. But Ryan didn't know that. Lizzie knew she had to do something, or Ryan would think that Miranda was a total freak! Lizzie struggled woozily to her feet.

Ryan frowned at Miranda. "Did you want to talk to me?"

"Uh," Miranda grunted. "I . . . uh . . . uh . . ."

i thought *i* was the one who got bumped on the head.

"I . . . um . . ." Miranda went on.

Lizzie decided that this was as good a place as any to jump in. "Uh, yeah, she did," Lizzie said quickly. "We, we, uh . . . we saw you in the drama class yesterday. And she just wanted to tell you that you, uh, you were amazing. Amazing. Yeah!" Lizzie grabbed Miranda's arm. "She wanted to say that you were amazing."

"Amazing," Miranda said mechanically. "Ryan. Amazing."

Ryan grinned, revealing two dimples in his cheeks. "Thanks."

The dimples seemed to have a hypnotic effect on Miranda.

"So . . ." Ryan said uncomfortably. "Well, I guess, I'll see you guys later." He walked off down the hall.

"What is wrong with you?" Lizzie whispered fiercely to Miranda, once Ryan was out of earshot. "You couldn't even talk to him? You were totally freaking me out."

"*You're* freaked out?" Miranda demanded. "I just reminded myself of *you* just now!"

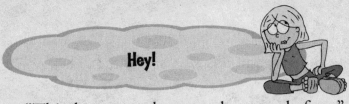

Hey!

"This has never happened to me before," Miranda said, wide-eyed as she and Lizzie started walking toward their next class. "What do I do?"

Lizzie shook her head. Honestly, she had no clue. How was Miranda supposed to get together with Ryan if she acted like a lobotomy patient whenever he was around? "Maybe you just got nervous," Lizzie said hopefully.

Miranda rolled her eyes. "Lizzie, this is me you're talking to," she said simply. "I don't get nervous. That's you."

Hey, again!

"Well, maybe you'll just have to try talking to him again," Lizzie suggested. "See what happens."

"I can't!" Miranda cried. "I choked! I stammered! I sweat!" She gestured wildly to herself. "I don't sweat!"

"Go!" Lizzie said, snapping her fingers at her friend. "Snap out of it!"

Miranda took a deep breath and shook her head. "This love stuff is freaky," she said.

Lizzie nodded. Tell me about it, she thought.

Sorry! That's the end of the sneak peek for now. But don't go nuclear! To read the rest, all you have to do is look for the next title in the Lizzie McGuire series—